John Ingerfield
and Other Stories

John Ingerfield and Other Stories

Jerome K. Jerome

MINT EDITIONS

John Ingerfield and Other Stories was first published in 1894.

This edition published by Mint Editions 2021.

ISBN 9781513278537 | E-ISBN 9781513278995

Published by Mint Editions®

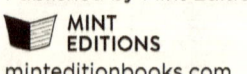 MINT
EDITIONS
minteditionbooks.com

Publishing Director: Jennifer Newens
Design & Production: Rachel Lopez Metzger
Project Manager: Micaela Clark
Typesetting: Westchester Publishing Services

Contents

To the Gentle Reader;
also To the Gentle Critic

Once upon a time, I wrote a little story of a woman who was crushed to death by a python. A day or two after its publication, a friend stopped me in the street. "Charming little story of yours," he said, "that about the woman and the snake; but it's not as funny as some of your things!" The next week, a newspaper, referring to the tale, remarked, "We have heard the incident related before with infinitely greater humour."

With this—and many similar experiences—in mind, I wish distinctly to state that "John Ingerfield," "The Woman of the Saeter," and "Silhouettes," are not intended to be amusing. The two other items—"Variety Patter," and "The Lease of the Cross Keys"—I give over to the critics of the new humour to rend as they will; but "John Ingerfield," "The Woman of the Saeter," and "Silhouettes," I repeat, I should be glad if they would judge from some other standpoint than that of humour, new or old.

In Remembrance of John Ingerfield, and of Anne, his Wife a Story of Old London, in Two Chapters

Chapter I

IF YOU TAKE THE UNDERGROUND Railway to Whitechapel Road (the East station), and from there take one of the yellow tramcars that start from that point, and go down the Commercial Road, past the George, in front of which starts—or used to stand—a high flagstaff, at the base of which sits—or used to sit—an elderly female purveyor of pigs' trotters at three-ha'pence apiece, until you come to where a railway arch crosses the road obliquely, and there get down and turn to the right up a narrow, noisy street leading to the river, and then to the right again up a still narrower street, which you may know by its having a public-house at one corner (as is in the nature of things) and a marine store-dealer's at the other, outside which strangely stiff and unaccommodating garments of gigantic size flutter ghost-like in the wind, you will come to a dingy railed-in churchyard, surrounded on all sides by cheerless, many-peopled houses. Sad-looking little old houses they are, in spite of the tumult of life about their ever open doors. They and the ancient church in their midst seem weary of the ceaseless jangle around them. Perhaps, standing there for so many years, listening to the long silence of the dead, the fretful voices of the living sound foolish in their ears.

Peering through the railings on the side nearest the river, you will see beneath the shadow of the soot-grimed church's soot-grimed porch—that is, if the sun happen, by rare chance, to be strong enough to cast any shadow at all in that region of grey light—a curiously high and narrow headstone that once was white and straight, not tottering and bent with age as it is now. There is upon this stone a carving in bas-relief, as you will see for yourself if you will make your way to it through the gateway on the opposite side of the square. It represents, so far as can be made out, for it is much worn by time and dirt, a figure lying on the ground with another figure bending over it, while at a little distance stands a third object. But this last is so indistinct that it might be almost anything, from an angel to a post.

And below the carving are the words (already half obliterated) that I have used for the title of this story.

Should you ever wander of a Sunday morning within sound of the cracked bell that calls a few habit-bound, old-fashioned folk to worship within those damp-stained walls, and drop into talk with the old men who on such days sometimes sit, each in his brass-buttoned long brown coat, upon the low stone coping underneath those broken railings, you might hear this tale from them, as I did, more years ago than I care to recollect.

But lest you do not choose to go to all this trouble, or lest the old men who could tell it you have grown tired of all talk, and are not to be roused ever again into the telling of tales, and you yet wish for the story, I will here set it down for you.

But I cannot recount it to you as they told it to me, for to me it was only a tale that I heard and remembered, thinking to tell it again for profit, while to them it was a thing that had been, and the threads of it were interwoven with the woof of their own life. As they talked, faces that I did not see passed by among the crowd and turned and looked at them, and voices that I did not hear spoke to them below the clamour of the street, so that through their thin piping voices there quivered the deep music of life and death, and my tale must be to theirs but as a gossip's chatter to the story of him whose breast has felt the press of battle.

JOHN INGERFIELD, OIL AND TALLOW refiner, of Lavender Wharf, Limehouse, comes of a hard-headed, hard-fisted stock. The first of the race that the eye of Record, piercing the deepening mists upon the centuries behind her, is able to discern with any clearness is a long-haired, sea-bronzed personage, whom men call variously Inge or Unger. Out of the wild North Sea he has come. Record observes him, one of a small, fierce group, standing on the sands of desolate Northumbria, staring landward, his worldly wealth upon his back. This consists of a two-handed battle-axe, value perhaps some forty stycas in the currency of the time. A careful man, with business capabilities, may, however, manipulate a small capital to great advantage. In what would appear, to those accustomed to our slow modern methods, an incredibly short space of time, Inge's two-handed battle-axe has developed into wide lands and many head of cattle; which latter continue to multiply with a rapidity beyond the dreams of present-day breeders. Inge's descendants would seem to have inherited the genius of their ancestor, for they prosper and their worldly goods increase. They are a money-making race. In all times, out of all things, by all means, they make money. They fight for money, marry for money, live for money, are ready to die for money.

In the days when the most saleable and the highest priced article in the markets of Europe was a strong arm and a cool head, then each Ingerfield (as "Inge," long rooted in Yorkshire soil, had grown or been corrupted to) was a soldier of fortune, and offered his strong arm and his cool head to the highest bidder. They fought for their price, and they took good care that they obtained their price; but, the price settled, they fought well, for they were staunch men and true, according to their lights, though these lights may have been placed somewhat low down, near the earth.

Then followed the days when the chief riches of the world lay tossed for daring hands to grasp upon the bosom of the sea, and the sleeping spirit of the old Norse Rover stirred in their veins, and the lilt of a wild sea-song they had never heard kept ringing in their ears; and they built them ships and sailed for the Spanish Main, and won much wealth, as was their wont.

Later on, when Civilisation began to lay down and enforce sterner rules for the game of life, and peaceful methods promised to prove more profitable than violent, the Ingerfields became traders and merchants of grave mien and sober life; for their ambition from generation to generation remains ever the same, their various callings being but means to an end.

A hard, stern race of men they would seem to have been, but just—so far as they understood justice. They have the reputation of having been good husbands, fathers, and masters; but one cannot help thinking of them as more respected than loved.

They were men to exact the uttermost farthing due to them, yet not without a sense of the thing due from them, their own duty and responsibility—nay, not altogether without their moments of heroism, which is the duty of great men. History relates how a certain Captain Ingerfield, returning with much treasure from the West Indies—how acquired it were, perhaps, best not to inquire too closely—is overhauled upon the high seas by King's frigate. Captain of King's frigate sends polite message to Captain Ingerfield requesting him to be so kind as to promptly hand over a certain member of his ship's company, who, by some means or another, has made himself objectionable to King's friends, in order that he (the said objectionable person) may be forthwith hanged from the yard-arm.

Captain Ingerfield returns polite answer to Captain of King's frigate that he (Captain Ingerfield) will, with much pleasure, hang any member of his ship's company that needs hanging, but that neither the King of England nor any one else on God Almighty's sea is going to do it for him. Captain of King's frigate sends back word that if objectionable person be not at once given up he shall be compelled with much regret to send Ingerfield and his ship to the bottom of the Atlantic. Replies Captain Ingerfield, "That is just what he will have to do before I give up one of my people," and fights the big frigate—fights it so fiercely that after three hours Captain of King's frigate thinks it will be good to try argument again, and sends therefore a further message, courteously acknowledging Captain Ingerfield's courage and skill, and suggesting that, he having done sufficient to vindicate his honour and renown, it would be politic to now hand over the unimportant cause of contention, and so escape with his treasure.

"Tell your Captain," shouts back this Ingerfield, who has discovered there are sweeter things to fight for than even money, "that the *Wild Goose* has flown the seas with her belly full of treasure before now, and will, if it be God's pleasure, so do again, but that master and man in her sail together, fight together, and die together."

Whereupon King's frigate pounds away more vigorously than ever, and succeeds eventually in carrying out her threat. Down goes the *Wild Goose*, her last chase ended—down she goes with a plunge, spit foremost with her colours flying; and down with her goes every man left standing on her decks; and at the bottom of the Atlantic they lie to this day, master and man side by side, keeping guard upon their treasure.

Which incident, and it is well authenticated, goes far to prove that the Ingerfields, hard men and grasping men though they be—men caring more for the getting of money than for the getting of love— loving more the cold grip of gold than the grip of kith or kin, yet bear buried in their hearts the seeds of a nobler manhood, for which, however, the barren soil of their ambition affords scant nourishment.

The John Ingerfield of this story is a man very typical of his race. He has discovered that the oil and tallow refining business, though not a pleasant one, is an exceedingly lucrative one. These are the good days when George the Third is king, and London is rapidly becoming a city of bright night. Tallow and oil and all materials akin thereto are in ever-growing request, and young John Ingerfield builds himself a large refining house and warehouse in the growing suburb of Limehouse, which lies between the teeming river and the quiet fields, gathers many people round about him, puts his strong heart into his work, and prospers.

All the days of his youth he labours and garners, and lays out and garners yet again. In early middle age he finds himself a wealthy man. The chief business of life, the getting of money, is practically done; his enterprise is firmly established, and will continue to grow with ever less need of husbandry. It is time for him to think about the secondary business of life, the getting together of a wife and home, for the Ingerfields have ever been good citizens, worthy heads of families, openhanded hosts, making a brave show among friends and neighbours.

John Ingerfield, sitting in his stiff, high-backed chair, in his stiffly, but solidly, furnished dining-room, above his counting-house, sipping slowly his one glass of port, takes counsel with himself.

What shall she be?

He is rich, and can afford a good article. She must be young and handsome, fit to grace the fine house he will take for her in fashionable Bloomsbury, far from the odour and touch of oil and tallow. She must be well bred, with a gracious, noble manner, that will charm his guests and reflect honour and credit upon himself; she must, above all, be of good family, with a genealogical tree sufficiently umbrageous to hide Lavender Wharf from the eyes of Society.

What else she may or may not be he does not very much care. She will, of course, be virtuous and moderately pious, as it is fit and proper that women should be. It will also be well that her disposition be gentle and yielding, but that is of minor importance, at all events so far as he is concerned: the Ingerfield husbands are not the class of men upon whom wives vent their tempers.

Having decided in his mind *what* she shall be, he proceeds to discuss with himself *who* she shall be. His social circle is small. Methodically, in thought, he makes the entire round of it, mentally scrutinising every maiden that he knows. Some are charming, some are fair, some are rich; but no one of them approaches near to his carefully considered ideal.

He keeps the subject in his mind, and muses on it in the intervals of business. At odd moments he jots down names as they occur to him upon a slip of paper, which he pins for the purpose on the inside of the cover of his desk. He arranges them alphabetically, and when it is as complete as his memory can make it, he goes critically down the list, making a few notes against each. As a result, it becomes clear to him that he must seek among strangers for his wife.

He has a friend, or rather an acquaintance, an old school-fellow, who has developed into one of those curious social flies that in all ages are to be met with buzzing contentedly within the most exclusive circles, and concerning whom, seeing that they are neither rare nor rich, nor extraordinarily clever nor well born, one wonders "how the devil they got there!" Meeting this man by chance one afternoon, he links his arm in his and invites him home to dinner.

So soon as they are left alone, with the walnuts and wine between them, John Ingerfield says, thoughtfully cracking a hard nut between his fingers—

"Will, I'm going to get married."

"Excellent idea—delighted to hear it, I'm sure," replies Will, somewhat less interested in the information than in the delicately flavoured Madeira he is lovingly sipping. "Who's the lady?"

"I don't know, yet," is John Ingerfield's answer.

His friend glances slyly at him over his glass, not sure whether he is expected to be amused or sympathetically helpful.

"I want you to find one for me."

Will Cathcart puts down his glass and stares at his host across the table.

"Should be delighted to help you, Jack," he stammers, in an alarmed tone—"'pon my soul I should; but really don't know a damned woman I could recommend—'pon my soul I don't."

"You must see a good many: I wish you'd look out for one that you *could* recommend."

"Certainly I will, my dear Jack!" answers the other, in a relieved voice. "Never thought about 'em in that way before. Daresay I shall come across the very girl to suit you. I'll keep my eyes open and let you know."

"I shall be obliged to you if you will," replies John Ingerfield, quietly; "and it's your turn, I think, to oblige me, Will. I have obliged you, if you recollect."

"Shall never forget it, my dear Jack," murmurs Will, a little uneasily. "It was uncommonly good of you. You saved me from ruin, Jack: shall think about it to my dying day—'pon my soul I shall."

"No need to let it worry you for so long a period as that," returns

John, with the faintest suspicion of a smile playing round his firm mouth. "The bill falls due at the end of next month. You can discharge the debt then, and the matter will be off your mind."

Will finds his chair growing uncomfortable under him, while the Madeira somehow loses its flavour. He gives a short, nervous laugh.

"By Jove," he says: "so soon as that? The date had quite slipped my memory."

"Fortunate that I reminded you," says John, the smile round his lips deepening.

Will fidgets on his seat. "I'm afraid, my dear Jack," he says, "I shall have to get you to renew it, just for a month or two,—deuced awkward thing, but I'm remarkably short of money this year. Truth is, I can't get what's owing to myself."

"That's very awkward, certainly," replies his friend, "because I am not at all sure that I shall be able to renew it."

Will stares at him in some alarm. "But what am I to do if I hav'n't the money?"

John Ingerfield shrugs his shoulders.

"You don't mean, my dear Jack, that you would put me in prison?"

"Why not? Other people have to go there who can't pay their debts."

Will Cathcart's alarm grows to serious proportions. "But our friendship," he cries, "our—"

"My dear Will," interrupts the other, "there are few friends I would lend three hundred pounds to and make no effort to get it back. You, certainly, are not one of them."

"Let us make a bargain," he continues. "Find me a wife, and on the day of my marriage I will send you back that bill with, perhaps, a couple of hundred added. If by the end of next month you have not introduced me to a lady fit to be, and willing to be, Mrs. John Ingerfield, I shall decline to renew it."

John Ingerfield refills his own glass and hospitably pushes the bottle towards his guest—who, however, contrary to his custom, takes no notice of it, but stares hard at his shoe-buckles.

"Are you serious?" he says at length.

"Quite serious," is the answer. "I want to marry. My wife must be a lady by birth and education. She must be of good family—of family sufficiently good, indeed, to compensate for the refinery. She must be young and beautiful and charming. I am purely a business man. I want a woman capable of conducting the social department of my life. I know of no such lady myself. I appeal to you, because you, I know, are intimate with the class among whom she must be sought."

"There may be some difficulty in persuading a lady of the required qualifications to accept the situation," says Cathcart, with a touch of malice.

"I want you to find one who will," says John Ingerfield.

Early in the evening Will Cathcart takes leave of his host, and departs thoughtful and anxious; and John Ingerfield strolls contemplatively up and down his wharf, for the smell of oil and tallow has grown to be very sweet to him, and it is pleasant to watch the moonbeams shining on the piled-up casks.

Six weeks go by. On the first day of the seventh John takes Will Cathcart's acceptance from its place in the large safe, and lays it in the smaller box beside his desk, devoted to more pressing and immediate business. Two days later Cathcart picks his way across the slimy yard, passes through the counting-house, and enters his friend's inner sanctum, closing the door behind him.

He wears a jubilant air, and slaps the grave John on the back. "I've got her, Jack," he cries. "It's been hard work, I can tell you: sounding suspicious old dowagers, bribing confidential servants, fishing for information among friends of the family. By Jove, I shall be able to join the Duke's staff as spy-in-chief to His Majesty's entire forces after this!"

"What is she like?" asks John, without stopping his writing.

"Like! My dear Jack, you'll fall over head and ears in love with her the moment you see her. A little cold, perhaps, but that will just suit you."

"Good family?" asks John, signing and folding the letter he has finished.

"So good that I was afraid at first it would be useless thinking of her. But she's a sensible girl, no confounded nonsense about her, and the family are poor as church mice. In fact—well, to tell the truth, we have become most excellent friends, and she told me herself frankly that she meant to marry a rich man, and didn't much care whom."

"That sounds hopeful," remarks the would-be bridegroom, with his peculiar dry smile: "when shall I have the pleasure of seeing her?"

"I want you to come with me to-night to the Garden," replies the other; "she will be in Lady Heatherington's box, and I will introduce you."

So that evening John Ingerfield goes to Covent Garden Theatre, with the blood running a trifle quicker in his veins, but not much, than would be the case were he going to the docks to purchase tallow—examines, covertly, the proposed article from the opposite side of the house, and approves her—is introduced to her, and, on closer inspection, approves her still more—receives an invitation to visit—visits frequently, and each time is more satisfied of the rarity, serviceableness, and quality of the article.

If all John Ingerfield requires for a wife is a beautiful social machine, surely here he has found his ideal. Anne Singleton, only daughter of that persistently unfortunate but most charming of baronets, Sir Harry Singleton (more charming, it is rumoured, outside his family circle than within it), is a stately graceful, high-bred woman. Her portrait, by Reynolds, still to be seen above the carved wainscoting of one of the old City halls, shows a wonderfully handsome and clever face, but at the same time a wonderfully cold and heartless one. It is the face of a woman half weary of, half sneering at the world. One reads in old family letters, whereof the ink is now very faded and the paper very yellow, long criticisms of this portrait. The writers complain that if the picture is at all like her she must have greatly changed since her girlhood, for they remember her then as having a laughing and winsome expression.

They say—they who knew her in after-life—that this earlier face came back to her in the end, so that the many who remembered opening their eyes and seeing her bending down over them could never recognise the portrait of the beautiful sneering lady, even when they were told whom it represented.

But at the time of John Ingerfield's strange wooing she was the Anne Singleton of Sir Joshua's portrait, and John Ingerfield liked her the better that she was.

He had no feeling of sentiment in the matter himself, and it simplified the case that she had none either. He offered her a plain bargain, and she accepted it. For all he knew or cared, her attitude towards this subject of marriage was the usual one assumed by women. Very young girls had their heads full of romantic ideas. It was better for her and for him that she had got rid of them.

"Ours will be a union founded on good sense," said John Ingerfield.

"Let us hope the experiment will succeed," said Anne Singleton.

Chapter II

BUT THE EXPERIMENT DOES NOT succeed. The laws of God decree that man shall purchase woman, that woman shall give herself to man, for other coin than that of good sense. Good sense is not a legal tender in the marriage mart. Men and women who enter therein with only sense in their purse have no right to complain if, on reaching home, they find they have concluded an unsatisfactory bargain.

John Ingerfield, when he asked Anne Singleton to be his wife, felt no more love for her than he felt for any of the other sumptuous household appointments he was purchasing about the same time, and made no pretence of doing so. Nor, had he done so, would she have believed him; for Anne Singleton has learned much in her twenty-two summers and winters, and knows that love is only a meteor in life's sky, and that the true lodestar of this world is gold. Anne Singleton has had her romance and buried it deep down in her deep nature and over its grave, to keep its ghost from rising, has piled the stones of indifference and contempt, as many a woman has done before and since. Once upon a time Anne Singleton sat dreaming out a story. It was a story old as the hills—older than some of them—but to her, then, it was quite new and very wonderful. It contained all the usual stock material common to such stories: the lad and the lass, the plighted troth, the richer suitors, the angry parents, the love that was worth braving all the world for. One day into this dream there fell from the land of the waking a letter, a poor, pitiful letter: "You know I love you and only you," it ran; "my heart will always be yours till I die. But my father threatens to stop my allowance, and, as you know, I have nothing of my own except debts. Some would call her handsome, but how can I think of her beside you? Oh, why was money ever let to come into the world to curse us?" with many other puzzling questions of a like character, and much severe condemnation of Fate and Heaven and other parties generally, and much self-commiseration.

Anne Singleton took long to read the letter. When she had finished it, and had read it through again, she rose, and, crushing it her hand, flung it in the fire with a laugh, and as the flame burnt up and died away felt that her life had died with it, not knowing that bruised hearts can heal.

So when John Ingerfield comes wooing, and speaks to her no word of love but only of money, she feels that here at last is a genuine voice that she can trust. Love of the lesser side of life is still left to her. It will be pleasant to be the wealthy mistress of a fine house, to give great receptions, to exchange the secret poverty of home for display and luxury. These things are offered to her on the very terms she would have suggested herself. Accompanied by love she would have refused them, knowing she could give none in return.

But a woman finds it one thing not to desire affection and another thing not to possess it. Day by day the atmosphere of the fine house in Bloomsbury grows cold and colder about her heart. Guests warm it at times for a few hours, then depart, leaving it chillier than before.

For her husband she attempts to feel indifference, but living creatures joined together cannot feel indifference for each other. Even two dogs in a leash are compelled to think of one another. A man and wife must love or hate, like or dislike, in degree as the bond connecting them is drawn tight or allowed to hang slack. By mutual desire their chains of wedlock have been fastened as loosely as respect for security will permit, with the happy consequence that her aversion to him does not obtrude itself beyond the limits of politeness.

Her part of the contract she faithfully fulfils, for the Singletons also have their code of honour. Her beauty, her tact, her charm, her influence, are devoted to his service—to the advancement of his position, the furtherance of his ambition. Doors that would otherwise remain closed she opens to him. Society, that would otherwise pass by with a sneer, sits round his table. His wishes and pleasures are hers. In all things she yields him wifely duty, seeks to render herself agreeable to him, suffers in silence his occasional caresses. Whatever was implied in the bargain, that she will perform to the letter.

He, on his side, likewise performs his part with businesslike conscientiousness—nay, seeing that the pleasing of her brings no personal gratification to himself—not without generosity. He is ever thoughtful of and deferential to her, awarding her at all times an unvarying courteousness that is none the less sincere for being studied. Her every expressed want is gratified, her every known distaste respected. Conscious of his presence being an oppression to her, he is even careful not to intrude it upon her oftener than is necessary.

At times he asks himself, somewhat pertinently, what he has gained by marriage—wonders whether this social race was quite the most interesting game he could have elected to occupy his leisure—wonders whether, after all, he would not have been happier over his counting-house than in these sumptuous, glittering rooms, where he always seems, and feels himself to be, the uninvited guest.

The only feeling that a closer intimacy has created in him for his wife is that of indulgent contempt. As there is no equality between man and woman, so there can be no respect. She is a different being. He must either look up to her as superior to himself, or down upon her as inferior. When a man does the former he is more or less in love, and love to John Ingerfield is an unknown emotion. Her beauty, her charm, her social tact—even while he makes use of them for his own purposes, he despises as the weapons of a weak nature.

So in their big, cold mansion John Ingerfield and Anne, his wife, sit far apart, strangers to one another, neither desiring to know the other nearer.

About his business he never speaks to her, and she never questions him. To compensate for the slight shrinkage of time he is able to devote to it, he becomes more strict and exacting; grows a harsher master to his people, a sterner creditor, a greedier dealer, squeezing the uttermost out of every one, feverish to grow richer, so that he may spend more upon the game that day by day he finds more tiresome and uninteresting.

And the piled-up casks upon his wharves increase and multiply; and on the dirty river his ships and barges lie in ever-lengthening lines; and round his greasy cauldrons sweating, witch-like creatures swarm in ever-denser numbers, stirring oil and tallow into gold.

Until one summer, from its nest in the far East, there flutters westward a foul thing. Hovering over Limehouse suburb, seeing it crowded and unclean, liking its fetid smell, it settles down upon it.

Typhus is the creature's name. At first it lurks there unnoticed, battening upon the rich, rank food it finds around it, until, grown too big to hide longer, it boldly shows its hideous head, and the white face of Terror runs swiftly through alley and street, crying as it runs, forces itself into John Ingerfield's counting-house, and tells its tale. John Ingerfield sits for a while thinking. Then he mounts his horse and rides home at as hard a pace as the condition of the streets will allow. In the hall he meets Anne going out, and stops her.

"Don't come too near me," he says quietly. "Typhus fever has broken out at Limehouse, and they say one can communicate it, even without having it oneself. You had better leave London for a few weeks. Go down to your father's: I will come and fetch you when it is all over."

He passes her, giving her a wide berth, and goes upstairs, where he remains for some minutes in conversation with his valet. Then, coming down, he remounts and rides off again.

After a little while Anne goes up into his room. His man is kneeling in the middle of the floor, packing a valise.

"Where are you to take it?" she asks.

"Down to the wharf, ma'am," answers the man: "Mr. Ingerfield is going to be there for a day or two."

Then Anne sits in the great empty drawing-room, and takes *her* turn at thinking.

John Ingerfield finds, on his return to Limehouse, that the evil has greatly increased during the short time he has been away. Fanned by fear and ignorance, fed by poverty and dirt, the scourge is spreading through the district like a fire. Long smouldering in secret, it has now burst forth at fifty different points at once. Not a street, not a court but has its "case." Over a dozen of John's hands are down with it already. Two more have sunk prostrate beside their work within the last hour. The panic grows grotesque. Men and women tear their clothes off, looking to see if they have anywhere upon them a rash or a patch of mottled skin, find that they have, or imagine that they have, and rush, screaming, half-undressed, into the street. Two men, meeting in a narrow passage, both rush back, too frightened to pass each other. A boy stoops down and scratches his leg—not an action that under ordinary circumstances would excite much surprise in that neighbourhood. In an instant there is a wild stampede from the room, the strong trampling on the weak in their eagerness to escape.

These are not the days of organised defence against disease. There are kind hearts and willing hands in London town, but they are not yet closely enough banded together to meet a swift foe such as this. There are hospitals and charities galore, but these are mostly in the City, maintained by the City Fathers for the exclusive benefit of poor citizens and members of the guilds. The few free hospitals are already over-crowded and ill-prepared. Squalid, outlying Limehouse, belonging to nowhere, cared for by nobody, must fight for itself.

John Ingerfield calls the older men together, and with their help attempts to instil some sense and reason into his terrified people. Standing on the step of his counting-house, and addressing as many of them as are not too scared to listen, he tells them of the danger of fear and of the necessity for calmness and courage.

"We must face and fight this thing like men," he cries, in that deep, din-conquering voice that has served the Ingerfields in good stead on many a steel-swept field, on many a storm-struck sea; "there must be no cowardly selfishness, no faint-hearted despair. If we've got to die we'll die; but please God we'll live. Anyhow, we will stick together, and help each other. I mean to stop here with you, and do what I can for you. None of my people shall want."

John Ingerfield ceases, and as the vibrations of his strong tones roll away a sweet voice from beside him rises clear and firm:—

"I have come down to be with you also, and to help my husband. I shall take charge of the nursing and tending of your sick, and I hope I shall be of some real use to you. My husband and I are so sorry for you in your trouble. I know you will be brave and patient. We will all do our best, and be hopeful."

He turns, half expecting to see only the empty air and to wonder at the delirium in his brain. She puts her hand in his, and their eyes meet; and in that moment, for the first time in their lives, these two see one another.

They speak no word. There is no opportunity for words. There is work to be done, and done quickly, and Anne grasps it with the greed of a woman long hungry for the joy of doing. As John watches her moving swiftly and quietly through the bewildered throng, questioning, comforting, gently compelling, the thought comes to him, Ought he to allow her to be here, risking her life for his people? followed by the thought, How is he going to prevent it? For in this hour the knowledge is born within him that Anne is not his property; that he and she are fellow hands taking their orders from the same Master; that though it be well for them to work together and help each other, they must not hinder one another.

As yet John does not understand all this. The idea is new and strange to him. He feels as the child in a fairy story on suddenly discovering that the trees and flowers has he passed by carelessly a thousand times can think and talk. Once he whispers to her of the labour and the danger, but she answers simply, "They are my people too, John: it is my work"; and he lets her have her way.

Anne has a true woman's instinct for nursing, and her strong sense stands her in stead of experience. A glance into one or two of the squalid dens where these people live tells her that if her patients are to be saved they must be nursed away from their own homes; and she determines to convert the large counting-house—a long, lofty room at the opposite end of the wharf to the refinery—into a temporary hospital. Selecting some seven or eight of the most reliable women to assist her, she proceeds to prepare it for its purpose. Ledgers might be volumes of poetry, bills of lading mere street ballads, for all the respect that is shown to them. The older clerks stand staring aghast, feeling that the end of all things is surely at hand, and that the universe is rushing down into space, until, their idleness being detected, they are themselves promptly impressed for the sacrilegious work, and made to assist in the demolition of their own temple.

Anne's commands are spoken very sweetly, and are accompanied by the sweetest of smiles; but they are nevertheless commands, and somehow it does not occur to any one to disobey them. John—stern, masterful, authoritative John, who has never been approached with anything more dictatorial than a timid request since he left Merchant Taylors' School nineteen years ago, who would have thought that something had suddenly gone wrong with the laws of Nature if he had been—finds himself hurrying along the street on his way to a druggist's shop, slackens his pace an instant to ask himself why and wherefore he is doing so, recollects that he was told to do so and to make haste back, marvels who could have dared to tell him to do anything and to make haste back, remembers that it was Anne, is not quite sure what to think about it, but hurries on. He "makes haste back," is praised for having been so quick, and feels pleased with himself; is sent off again in another direction, with instructions what to say when he gets there. He starts off (he is becoming used to being ordered about now). Halfway there great alarm seizes him, for on attempting to say over the message to himself, to be sure that he has it quite right, he discovers he has forgotten it. He pauses, nervous and excited; cogitates as to whether it will be safe for him to concoct a message of his own, weighs anxiously the chances—supposing that he does so—of being found out. Suddenly, to his intense surprise and relief, every word of what he was told to say comes back to him; and he hastens on, repeating it over and over to himself as he walks, lest it should escape him again.

And then a few hundred yards farther on there occurs one of the most extraordinary events that has ever happened in that street before or since: John Ingerfield laughs.

John Ingerfield, of Lavender Wharf, after walking two-thirds of Creek Lane, muttering to himself with his eyes on the ground, stops in the middle of the road and laughs; and one small boy, who tells the story to his dying day, sees him and hears him, and runs home at the top of his speed with the wonderful news, and is conscientiously slapped by his mother for telling lies.

All that day Anne works like a heroine, John helping her, and occasionally getting in the way. By night she has her little hospital prepared and three beds already up and occupied; and, all now done that can be done, she and John go upstairs to his old rooms above the counting-house.

John ushers her into them with some misgiving, for by contrast with the house at Bloomsbury they are poor and shabby. He places her in the arm-chair near the fire, begging her to rest quiet, and then assists his old housekeeper, whose wits, never of the strongest, have been scared by the day's proceeding, to lay the meal.

Anne's eyes follow him as he moves about the room. Perhaps here, where all the real part of his life has been passed, he is more his true self than amid the unfamiliar surroundings of fashion; perhaps this simpler frame shows him to greater advantage; but Anne wonders how it is she has never noticed before that he is a well-set, handsome man. Nor, indeed, is he so very old-looking. Is it a trick of the dim light, or what? He looks almost young. But why should he not look young, seeing he is only thirty-six, and at thirty-six a man is in his prime? Anne wonders why she has always thought of him as an elderly person.

A portrait of one of John's ancestors hangs over the great mantelpiece—of that sturdy Captain Ingerfield who fought the King's frigate rather than give up one of his people. Anne glances from the dead face to the living and notes the strong likeness between them. Through her half-closed eyes she sees the grim old captain hurling back his message of defiance, and his face is the face she saw a few hours ago, saying, "I mean to stop here with you and do what I can for you. None of my people shall want."

John is placing a chair for her at the table, and the light from the candles falls upon him. She steals another glance at his face—a strong, stern, handsome face, capable of becoming a noble face. Anne wonders if it has ever looked down tenderly at anyone; feels a sudden fierce pain at the thought; dismisses the thought as impossible; wonders, nevertheless, how tenderness would suit it; thinks she would like to see a look of tenderness upon it, simply out of curiosity; wonders if she ever will.

She rouses herself from her reverie as John, with a smile, tells her supper is ready, and they seat themselves opposite each other, an odd air of embarrassment pervading.

Day by day their work grows harder; day by day the foe grows stronger, fiercer, more all-conquering; and day by day, fighting side by side against it, John Ingerfield and Anne, his wife, draw closer to each other. On the battle-field of life we learn the worth of strength. Anne feels it good, when growing weary, to glance up and find him near her; feels it good, amid the troubled babel round her, to hear the deep, strong music of his voice.

And John, watching Anne's fair figure moving to and fro among the stricken and the mourning; watching her fair, fluttering hands, busy with their holy work, her deep, soul-haunting eyes, changeful with the light and shade of tenderness; listening to her sweet, clear voice, laughing with the joyous, comforting the comfortless, gently commanding, softly pleading, finds creeping into his brain strange new thoughts concerning women—concerning this one woman in particular.

One day, rummaging over an old chest, he comes across a coloured picture-book of Bible stories. He turns the torn pages fondly, remembering the Sunday afternoons of long ago. At one picture, wherein are represented many angels, he pauses; for in one of the younger angels of the group—one not quite so severe of feature as her sisters—he fancies he can trace resemblance to Anne. He lingers long over it. Suddenly there rushes through his brain the thought, How good to stoop and kiss the sweet feet of such a woman! and, thinking it, he blushes like a boy.

So from the soil of human suffering spring the flowers of human love and joy, and from the flowers there fall the seeds of infinite pity for human pain, God shaping all things to His ends.

Thinking of Anne, John's face grows gentler, his hand kinder; dreaming of him, her heart grows stronger, deeper, fuller. Every available room in the warehouse has been turned into a ward, and the little hospital is open free to all, for John and Anne feel that the whole world are their people. The piled-up casks are gone—shipped to Woolwich and Gravesend, bundled anywhere out of the way, as though oil and tallow and the gold they can be stirred into were matters of small moment in this world, not to be thought of beside such a thing as the helping of a human brother in sore strait.

All the labour of the day seems light to them, looking forward to the hour when they sit together in John's old shabby dining-room above the counting-house. Yet a looker-on might imagine such times dull to them; for they are strangely shy of one another, strangely sparing of words—fearful of opening the flood-gates of speech, feeling the pressure of the pent-up thought.

One evening, John, throwing out words, not as a sop to the necessity for talk, but as a bait to catch Anne's voice, mentions girdle-cakes, remembers that his old housekeeper used to be famous for the making of them, and wonders if she has forgotten the art.

Anne, answering tremulously, as though girdle-cakes were a somewhat delicate topic, claims to be a successful amateur of them herself. John, having been given always to understand that the talent for them was exceedingly rare, and one usually hereditary, respectfully doubts Anne's capabilities, deferentially suggesting that she is thinking of scones. Anne indignantly repudiates the insinuation, knows quite well the difference between girdle-cakes and scones, offers to prove her powers by descending into the kitchen and making some then and there, if John will accompany her and find the things for her.

John accepts the challenge, and, guiding Anne with one shy, awkward hand, while holding aloft a candle in the other, leads the way. It is past ten o'clock, and the old housekeeper is in bed. At each creaking stair they pause, to listen if the noise has awakened her; then, finding all silent, creep forward again, with suppressed laughter, wondering with alarm, half feigned, half real, what the prim, methodical dame would say were she to come down and catch them.

They reach the kitchen, thanks more to the suggestions of a friendly cat than to John's acquaintanceship with the geography of his own house; and Anne rakes together the fire and clears the table for her work. What possible use John is to her—what need there was for her stipulating that he should accompany her, Anne might find it difficult, if examined, to explain satisfactorily. As for his "finding the things" for her, he has not the faintest notion where they are, and possesses no natural aptitude for discovery. Told to find flour, he industriously searches for it in the dresser drawers; sent for the rolling-pin—the nature and characteristics of rolling-pins being described to him for his guidance—he returns, after a prolonged absence, with the copper stick. Anne laughs at him; but really it would seem as though she herself were almost as stupid, for not until her hands are covered with flour does it occur to her that she has not taken that preliminary step in all cooking operations of rolling up her sleeves.

She holds out her arms to John, first one and then the other, asking him sweetly if he minds doing it for her. John is very slow and clumsy, but Anne stands very patient. Inch by inch he peels the black sleeve from the white round arm. Hundreds of times must he have seen those fair arms, bare to the shoulder, sparkling with jewels; but never before has he seen their wondrous beauty. He longs to clasp them round his neck, yet is fearful lest his trembling fingers touching them as he performs his tantalising task may offend her. Anne thanks him, and apologises for having given him so much trouble, and he murmurs some meaningless reply, and stands foolishly silent, watching her.

Anne seems to find one hand sufficient for her cake-making, for the other rests idly on the table—very near to one of John's, as she would see were not her eyes so intent upon her work. How the impulse came to him, where he—grave, sober, business-man John—learnt such story-book ways can never be known; but in one instant he is down on both knees, smothering the floury hand with kisses, and the next moment Anne's arms are round his neck and her lips against his, and the barrier between them is swept away, and the deep waters of their love rush together.

With that kiss they enter a new life whereinto one may not follow them. One thinks it must have been a life made strangely beautiful by self-forgetfulness, strangely sweet by mutual devotion—a life too ideal, perhaps, to have remained for long undimmed by the mists of earth.

They who remember them at that time speak of them in hushed tones, as one speaks of visions. It would almost seem as though from their faces in those days there shone a radiance, as though in their voices dwelt a tenderness beyond the tenderness of man.

They seem never to rest, never to weary. Day and night, through that little stricken world, they come and go, bearing healing and peace, till at last the plague, like some gorged beast of prey, slinks slowly back towards its lair, and men raise their heads and breathe.

One afternoon, returning from a somewhat longer round than usual, John feels a weariness creeping into his limbs, and quickens his step, eager to reach home and rest. Anne, who has been up all the previous night, is asleep, and not wishing to disturb her, he goes into the dining-room and sits down in the easy chair before the fire. The room strikes cold. He stirs the logs, but they give out no greater heat. He draws his chair right in front of them, and sits leaning over them with his feet on the hearth and his hands outstretched towards the blaze; yet he still shivers.

Twilight fills the room and deepens into dusk. He wonders listlessly how it is that Time seems to be moving with such swift strides. After a while he hears a voice close to him, speaking in a slow, monotonous tone—a voice curiously familiar to him, though he cannot tell to whom it belongs. He does not turn his head, but sits listening to it drowsily. It is talking about tallow: one hundred and ninety-four casks of tallow, and they must all stand one inside the other. It cannot be done, the voice complains pathetically. They will not go inside each other. It is no good pushing them. See! they only roll out again.

The voice grows wearily fretful. Oh! why do they persist when they see it is impossible? What fools they all are!

Suddenly he recollects the voice, and starts up and stares wildly about him, trying to remember where he is. With a fierce straining of his will he grips the brain that is slipping away from him, and holds it. As soon as he feels sure of himself he steals out of the room and down the stairs.

In the hall he stands listening; the house is very silent. He goes to the head of the stairs leading to the kitchen and calls softly to the old housekeeper, and she comes up to him, panting and grunting as she climbs each step. Keeping some distance from her, he asks in a whisper where Anne is. The woman answers that she is in the hospital.

"Tell her I have been called away suddenly on business," he says, speaking in quick, low tones: "I shall be away for some days. Tell her to leave here and return home immediately. They can do without her here now. Tell her to go back home at once. I will join her there."

He moves toward the door but stops and faces round again.

"Tell her I beg and entreat her not to stop in this place an hour longer. There is nothing to keep her now. It is all over: there is nothing that cannot be done by any one. Tell her she must go home—this very night. Tell her if she loves me to leave this place at once."

The woman, a little bewildered by his vehemence, promises, and disappears down the stairs. He takes his hat and cloak from the chair on which he had thrown them, and turns once more to cross the hall. As he does so, the door opens and Anne enters.

He darts back into the shadow, squeezing himself against the wall. Anne calls to him laughingly, then, as he does not answer, with a frightened accent:

"John,—John, dear. Was not that you? Are not you there?"

He holds his breath, and crouches still closer into the dark corner;

and Anne, thinking she must have been mistaken in the dim light, passes him and goes upstairs.

Then he creeps stealthily to the door, lets himself out and closes it softly behind him.

After the lapse of a few minutes the old housekeeper plods upstairs and delivers John's message. Anne, finding it altogether incomprehensible, subjects the poor dame to severe examination, but fails to elicit anything further. What is the meaning of it? What "business" can have compelled John, who for ten weeks has never let the word escape his lips, to leave her like this—without a word! without a kiss! Then suddenly she remembers the incident of a few moments ago, when she had called to him, thinking she saw him, and he did not answer; and the whole truth strikes her full in the heart.

She refastens the bonnet-strings she has been slowly untying, and goes down and out into the wet street.

She makes her way rapidly to the house of the only doctor resident in the neighbourhood—a big, brusque-mannered man, who throughout these terrible two months has been their chief stay and help. He meets her on her entrance with an embarrassed air that tells its own tale, and at once renders futile his clumsy attempts at acting:—

How should he know where John is? Who told her John had the fever—a great, strong, hulking fellow like that? She has been working too hard, and has got fever on the brain. She must go straight back home, or she will be having it herself. She is more likely to take it than John.

Anne, waiting till he has finished jerking out sentences while stamping up and down the room, says gently, taking no notice of his denials,—"If you will not tell me I must find out from some one else—that is all." Then, her quick eyes noting his momentary hesitation, she lays her little hand on his rough paw, and, with the shamelessness of a woman who loves deeply, wheedles everything out of him that he has promised to keep secret.

He stops her, however, as she is leaving the room. "Don't go in to him now," he says; "he will worry about you. Wait till to-morrow."

So, while John lies counting endless casks of tallow, Anne sits by his side, tending her last "case."

Often in his delirium he calls her name, and she takes his fevered hand in hers and holds it, and he falls asleep.

Each morning the doctor comes and looks at him, asks a few questions and gives a few commonplace directions, but makes no comment. It would be idle his attempting to deceive her.

The days move slowly through the darkened room. Anne watches his thin hands grow thinner, his sunken eyes grow bigger; yet remains strangely calm, almost contented.

Very near the end there comes an hour when John wakes as from a dream, and remembers all things clearly.

He looks at her half gratefully, half reproachfully.

"Anne, why are you here?" he asks, in a low, laboured voice. "Did they not give you my message?"

For answer she turns her deep eyes upon him.

"Would you have gone away and left me here to die?" she questions him, with a faint smile.

She bends her head down nearer to him, so that her soft hair falls about his face.

"Our lives were one, dear," she whispers to him. "I could not have lived without you; God knew that. We shall be together always."

She kisses him, and laying his head upon her breast, softly strokes it as she might a child's; and he puts his weak arms around her.

Later on she feels them growing cold about her, and lays him gently back upon the bed, looks for the last time into his eyes, then draws the lids down over them.

His people ask that they may bury him in the churchyard hard by, so that he may always be among them; and, Anne consenting, they do all things needful with their own hands, wishful that no unloving labour may be mingled with their work. They lay him close to the porch, where, going in and out the church, their feet will pass near to him; and one among them who is cunning with the graver's chisel shapes the stone.

At the head he carves in bas-relief the figure of the good Samaritan tending the brother fallen by the way, and underneath the letters, "In Remembrance of John Ingerfield."

He thinks to put a verse of Scripture immediately after; but the gruff doctor says, "Better leave a space, in case you want to add another name."

So the stone remains a little while unfinished; till the same hand carves thereon, a few weeks later, "And of Anne, his Wife."

The Woman of the Saeter

Wild-reindeer stalking is hardly so exciting a sport as the evening's verandah talk in Norroway hotels would lead the trustful traveller to suppose. Under the charge of your guide, a very young man with the dreamy, wistful eyes of those who live in valleys, you leave the farmstead early in the forenoon, arriving towards twilight at the desolate hut which, for so long as you remain upon the uplands, will be your somewhat cheerless headquarters.

Next morning, in the chill, mist-laden dawn, you rise; and, after a breakfast of coffee and dried fish, shoulder your Remington, and step forth silently into the raw, damp air; the guide locking the door behind you, the key grating harshly in the rusty lock.

For hour after hour you toil over the steep, stony ground, or wind through the pines, speaking in whispers, lest your voice reach the quick ears of your prey, that keeps its head ever pressed against the wind. Here and there, in the hollows of the hills lie wide fields of snow, over which you pick your steps thoughtfully, listening to the smothered thunder of the torrent, tunnelling its way beneath your feet, and wondering whether the frozen arch above it be at all points as firm as is desirable. Now and again, as in single file you walk cautiously along some jagged ridge, you catch glimpses of the green world, three thousand feet below you; though you gaze not long upon the view, for your attention is chiefly directed to watching the footprints of the guide, lest by deviating to the right or left you find yourself at one stride back in the valley—or, to be more correct, are found there.

These things you do, and as exercise they are healthful and invigorating. But a reindeer you never see, and unless, overcoming the prejudices of your British-bred conscience, you care to take an occasional pop at a fox, you had better have left your rifle at the hut, and, instead, have brought a stick which would have been helpful. Notwithstanding which the guide continues sanguine, and in broken English, helped out by stirring gesture, tells of the terrible slaughter generally done by sportsmen under his superintendence, and of the vast herds that generally infest these fields; and when you grow sceptical upon the subject of Reins he whispers alluringly of Bears.

Once in a way you will come across a track, and will follow it breathlessly for hours, and it will lead to a sheer precipice. Whether the explanation is suicide, or a reprehensible tendency on the part of the animal towards practical joking, you are left to decide for yourself. Then, with many rough miles between you and your rest, you abandon the chase.

But I speak from personal experience merely.

All day long we had tramped through the pitiless rain, stopping only for an hour at noon to eat some dried venison and smoke a pipe beneath the shelter of an overhanging cliff. Soon afterwards Michael knocked over a ryper (a bird that will hardly take the trouble to hop out of your way) with his gun-barrel, which incident cheered us a little; and, later on, our flagging spirits were still further revived by the discovery of apparently very recent deer-tracks. These we followed, forgetful, in our eagerness, of the lengthening distance back to the hut, of the fading daylight, of the gathering mist. The track led us higher and higher, farther and farther into the mountains, until on the shores of a desolate rock-bound vand it abruptly ended, and we stood staring at one another, and the snow began to fall.

Unless in the next half-hour we could chance upon a saeter, this meant passing the night upon the mountain. Michael and I looked at the guide; but though, with characteristic Norwegian sturdiness, he put a bold face upon it, we could see that in that deepening darkness he knew no more than we did. Wasting no time on words, we made straight for the nearest point of descent, knowing that any human habitation must be far below us.

Down we scrambled, heedless of torn clothes and bleeding hands, the darkness pressing closer round us. Then suddenly it became black—black as pitch—and we could only hear each other. Another step might mean death. We stretched out our hands, and felt each other. Why we spoke in whispers, I do not know, but we seemed afraid of our own voices. We agreed there was nothing for it but to stop where we were till morning, clinging to the short grass; so we lay there side by side, for what may have been five minutes or may have been an hour. Then, attempting to turn, I lost my grip and rolled. I made convulsive efforts to clutch the ground, but the incline was too steep. How far I fell I could not say, but at last something stopped me. I felt it cautiously with my foot: it did not yield, so I twisted myself round and touched it with my hand. It seemed planted firmly in the earth. I passed my arm along to the right, then to the left. I shouted with joy. It was a fence.

Rising and groping about me, I found an opening, and passed through, and crept forward with palms outstretched until I touched

JEROME K. JEROME

the logs of a hut; then, feeling my way round, discovered the door, and knocked. There came no response, so I knocked louder; then pushed, and the heavy woodwork yielded, groaning. But the darkness within was even darker than the darkness without. The others had contrived to crawl down and join me. Michael struck a wax vesta and held it up, and slowly the room came out of the darkness and stood round us.

Then something rather startling happened. Giving one swift glance about him, our guide uttered a cry, and rushed out into the night. We followed to the door, and called after him, but only a voice came to us out of the blackness, and the only words that we could catch, shrieked back in terror, were: "*Saetervronen! Saetervronen!*" ("The woman of the saeter").

"Some foolish superstition about the place, I suppose," said Michael. "In these mountain solitudes men breed ghosts for company. Let us make a fire. Perhaps, when he sees the light, his desire for food and shelter may get the better of his fears."

We felt about in the small enclosure round the house, and gathered juniper and birch-twigs, and kindled a fire upon the open stove built in the corner of the room. Fortunately, we had some dried reindeer and bread in our bag, and on that and the ryper and the contents of our flasks we supped. Afterwards, to while away the time, we made an inspection of the strange eyrie we had lighted on.

It was an old log-built saeter. Some of these mountain farmsteads are as old as the stone ruins of other countries. Carvings of strange beasts and demons were upon its blackened rafters, and on the lintel, in runic letters, ran this legend: "Hund builded me in the days of Haarfager." The house consisted of two large apartments. Originally, no doubt, these had been separate dwellings standing beside one another, but they were now connected by a long, low gallery. Most of the scanty furniture was almost as ancient as the walls themselves, but many articles of a comparatively recent date had been added. All was now, however, rotting and falling into decay.

The place appeared to have been deserted suddenly by its last occupants. Household utensils lay as they were left, rust and dirt encrusted on them. An open book, limp and mildewed, lay face downwards on the table, while many others were scattered about both rooms, together with much paper, scored with faded ink. The curtains hung in shreds about the windows; a woman's cloak, of an antiquated fashion, drooped from a nail behind the door. In an oak chest we found a tumbled heap of yellow letters. They were of various dates, extending over a period of four months; and with them, apparently intended to receive them, lay a large envelope, inscribed with an address in London that has since disappeared.

Strong curiosity overcoming faint scruples, we read them by the dull glow of the burning juniper twigs, and, as we lay aside the last of them, there rose from the depths below us a wailing cry, and all night long it rose and died away, and rose again, and died away again; whether born of our brain or of some human thing, God knows.

And these, a little altered and shortened, are the letters:—
Extract from first letter:

"I cannot tell you, my dear Joyce, what a haven of peace this place is to me after the racket and fret of town. I am almost quite recovered already, and am growing stronger every day; and, joy of joys, my brain has come back to me, fresher and more vigorous, I think, for its holiday. In this silence and solitude my thoughts flow freely, and the difficulties of my task are disappearing as if by magic. We are perched upon a tiny plateau halfway up the mountain. On one side the rock rises almost perpendicularly, piercing the sky; while on the other, two thousand feet below us, the torrent hurls itself into the black waters of the fiord. The house consists of two rooms—or, rather, it is two cabins connected by a passage. The larger one we use as a living room, and the other is our sleeping apartment. We have no servant, but do everything for ourselves. I fear sometimes Muriel must find it lonely. The nearest human habitation is eight miles away, across the mountain, and not a soul comes near us. I spend as much time as I can with her, however, during the day, and make up for it by working at night after she has gone to sleep; and when I question her, she only laughs, and answers that she loves to have me all to herself. (Here you will smile cynically, I know, and say, 'Humph, I wonder will she say the same when they have been married six years instead of six months.') At the rate I am working now I shall have finished my first volume by the spring, and then, my dear fellow, you must try and come over, and we will walk and talk together 'amid these storm-reared temples of the gods.' I have felt a new man since I arrived here. Instead of having to 'cudgel my brains,' as we say, thoughts crowd upon me. This work will make my name."

Part of the third letter, the second being mere talk about the book (a history apparently) that the man was writing:

My Dear Joyce,

I have written you two letters—this will make the third—but have been unable to post them. Every day I have been expecting a visit from some farmer or villager, for the Norwegians are kindly people towards strangers—to say nothing of the inducements of trade. A fortnight having passed, however, and the commissariat question having become serious, I yesterday set out before dawn, and made my way down to the valley; and this gives me something to tell you. Nearing the village, I met a peasant woman. To my intense surprise, instead of returning my salutation, she stared at me, as if I were some wild animal, and shrank away from me as far as the width of the road would permit. In the village the same experience awaited me. The children ran from me, the people avoided me. At last a grey- haired old man appeared to take pity on me, and from him I learnt the explanation of the mystery. It seems there is a strange superstition attaching to this house in which we are living. My things were brought up here by the two men who accompanied me from Drontheim, but the natives are afraid to go near the place, and prefer to keep as far as possible from any one connected with it.

"The story is that the house was built by one Hund, 'a maker of runes' (one of the old saga writers, no doubt), who lived here with his young wife. All went peacefully until, unfortunately for him, a certain maiden stationed at a neighbouring saeter grew to love him.

"Forgive me if I am telling you what you know, but a 'saeter' is the name given to the upland pastures to which, during the summer, are sent the cattle, generally under the charge of one or more of the maids. Here for three months these girls will live in their lonely huts, entirely shut off from the world. Customs change little in this land. Two or three such stations are within climbing distance of this house, at this day, looked after by the farmers' daughters, as in the days of Hund, 'maker of runes.'

"Every night, by devious mountain paths, the woman would come and tap lightly at Hund's door. Hund had built himself two cabins, one behind the other (these are now, as I think I have explained to you, connected by a passage); the smaller one was the homestead; in the other he carved and wrote, so that while the young wife slept the 'maker of runes' and the saeter woman sat whispering.

"One night, however, the wife learnt all things, but said no word. Then, as now, the ravine in front of the enclosure was crossed by a slight bridge of planks, and over this bridge the woman of the saeter passed and repassed each night. On a day when Hund had gone down to fish in the fiord, the wife took an axe, and hacked and hewed at the bridge, yet it still looked firm and solid; and that night, as Hund sat waiting in his workshop, there struck upon his ears a piercing cry, and a crashing of logs and rolling rock, and then again the dull roaring of the torrent far below.

"But the woman did not die unavenged; for that winter a man, skating far down the fiord, noticed a curious object embedded in the ice; and when, stooping, he looked closer, he saw two corpses, one gripping the other by the throat, and the bodies were the bodies of Hund and his young wife.

"Since then, they say, the woman of the saeter haunts Hund's house, and if she sees a light within she taps upon the door, and no man may keep her out. Many, at different times, have tried to occupy the house, but strange tales are told of them. 'Men do not live at Hund's saeter,' said my old grey-haired friend, concluding his tale,—'they die there.'

"I have persuaded some of the braver of the villagers to bring what provisions and other necessaries we require up to a plateau about a mile from the house and leave them there. That is the most I have been able to do. It comes somewhat as a shock to one to find men and women—fairly educated and intelligent as many of them are—slaves to fears that one would expect a child to laugh at. But there is no reasoning with superstition."

Extract from the same letter, but from a part seemingly written a day or two later:

"At home I should have forgotten such a tale an hour after I had heard it, but these mountain fastnesses seem strangely fit to be the last stronghold of the supernatural. The woman haunts me already. At night instead of working, I find myself listening for her tapping at the door; and yesterday an incident occurred that makes me fear for my own common sense. I had gone out for a long walk alone, and the twilight was thickening into darkness as I neared home. Suddenly looking up from my reverie, I saw, standing on a knoll the other side of the ravine, the figure of a woman. She held a cloak about her head, and I could not see her face. I took off my cap, and called out a good-night to her, but she never moved or spoke. Then—God knows why, for my brain was full of other thoughts at the time—a clammy chill crept over me, and my tongue grew dry and parched. I stood rooted to the spot, staring at her across the yawning gorge that divided us; and slowly she moved away, and passed into the gloom, and I continued my way. I have said nothing to Muriel, and shall not. The effect the story has had upon myself warns me not to do so."

From a letter dated eleven days later:

"She has come. I have known she would, since that evening I saw her on the mountain; and last night she came, and we have sat and looked into each other's eyes. You will say, of course, that I am mad—that I have not recovered from my fever—that I have been working too hard—that I have heard a foolish tale, and that it has filled my overstrung brain with foolish fancies: I have told myself all that. But the thing came, nevertheless—a creature of flesh and blood? a creature of air? a creature of my own imagination?—what matter? it was real to me.

"It came last night, as I sat working, alone. Each night I have waited for it, listened for it—longed for it, I know now. I heard the passing of its feet upon the bridge, the tapping of its hand upon the door, three times—tap, tap, tap. I felt my loins grow cold, and a pricking pain about my head; and I gripped my chair with both hands, and waited, and again there came the tapping—tap, tap, tap. I rose and slipped the bolt of the door leading to the other room, and again I waited, and again there came the tapping—tap, tap, tap. Then I opened the heavy outer door, and the wind rushed past me, scattering my papers, and the woman entered in, and I closed the door behind her. She threw her hood back from her head, and unwound a kerchief from about her neck, and laid it on the table. Then she crossed and sat before the fire, and I noticed her bare feet were damp with the night dew.

"I stood over against her and gazed at her, and she smiled at me—a strange, wicked smile, but I could have laid my soul at her feet. She never spoke or moved, and neither did I feel the need of spoken words, for I understood the meaning of those upon the Mount when they said, 'Let us make here tabernacles: it is good for us to be here.'

"How long a time passed thus I do not know, but suddenly the woman held her hand up, listening, and there came a faint sound from the other room. Then swiftly she drew her hood about her face and passed out, closing the door softly behind her; and I drew back the bolt of the inner door and waited, and hearing nothing more, sat down, and must have fallen asleep in my chair.

"I awoke, and instantly there flashed through my mind the thought of the kerchief the woman had left behind her, and I started from my chair to hide it. But the table was already laid for breakfast, and my wife sat with her elbows on the table and her head between her hands, watching me with a look in her eyes that was new to me.

"She kissed me, though her lips were cold; and I argued to myself that the whole thing must have been a dream. But later in the day, passing the open door when her back was towards me, I saw her take the kerchief from a locked chest and look at it.

"I have told myself it must have been a kerchief of her own, and that all the rest has been my imagination; that, if not, then my strange visitant was no spirit, but a woman; and that, if human thing knows human thing, it was no creature of flesh and blood that sat beside me last night. Besides, what woman would she be? The nearest saeter is a three-hours' climb to a strong man, and the paths are dangerous even in daylight: what woman would have found them in the night? What woman would have chilled the air around her, and have made the blood flow cold through all my veins? Yet if she come again I will speak to her. I will stretch out my hand and see whether she be mortal thing or only air."

The fifth letter:

My Dear Joyce,

Whether your eyes will ever see these letters is doubtful. From this place I shall never send them. They would read to you as the ravings of a madman. If ever I return to England I may one day show them to you, but when I do it will be when I, with you, can laugh over them. At present I write them merely to hide away,—putting the words down on paper saves my screaming them aloud.

"She comes each night now, taking the same seat beside the embers, and fixing upon me those eyes, with the hell-light in them, that burn into my brain; and at rare times she smiles, and all my being passes out of me, and is hers. I make no attempt to work. I sit listening for her footsteps on the creaking bridge, for the rustling of her feet upon the grass, for the tapping of her hand upon the door. No word is uttered between us. Each day I say: 'When she comes to-night I will speak to her. I will stretch out my hand and touch her.' Yet when she enters, all thought and will goes out from me.

"Last night, as I stood gazing at her, my soul filled with her wondrous beauty as a lake with moonlight, her lips parted, and she started from her chair; and, turning, I thought I saw a white face pressed against the window, but as I looked it vanished. Then she drew her cloak about her, and passed out. I slid back the bolt I always draw now, and stole into the other room, and, taking down the lantern, held it above the bed. But Muriel's eyes were closed as if in sleep."

Extract from the sixth letter:

"It is not the night I fear, but the day. I hate the sight of this woman with whom I live, whom I call 'wife.' I shrink from the blow of her cold lips, the curse of her stony eyes. She has seen, she has learnt; I feel it, I know it. Yet she winds her arms around my neck, and calls me sweetheart, and smoothes my hair with her soft, false hands. We speak mocking words of love to one another, but I know her cruel eyes are ever following me. She is plotting her revenge, and I hate her, I hate her, I hate her!"

Part of the seventh letter:

"This morning I went down to the fiord. I told her I should not be back until the evening. She stood by the door watching me until we were mere specks to one another, and a promontory of the mountain shut me from view. Then, turning aside from the track, I made my way, running and stumbling over the jagged ground, round to the other side of the mountain, and began to climb again. It was slow, weary work. Often I had to go miles out of my road to avoid a ravine, and twice I reached a high point only to have to descend again. But at length I crossed the ridge, and crept down to a spot from where, concealed, I could spy upon my own house. She—my wife—stood by the flimsy bridge. A short hatchet, such as butchers use, was in her hand. She leant against a pine trunk, with her arm behind her, as one stands whose back aches with long stooping in some cramped position; and even at that distance I could see the cruel smile about her lips.

"Then I recrossed the ridge, and crawled down again, and, waiting until evening, walked slowly up the path. As I came in view of the house she saw me, and waved her handkerchief to me, and in answer I waved my hat, and shouted curses at her that the wind whirled away into the torrent. She met me with a kiss, and I breathed no hint to her that I had seen. Let her devil's work remain undisturbed. Let it prove to me what manner of thing this is that haunts me. If it be a spirit, then the bridge wilt bear it safely; if it be woman—

"But I dismiss the thought. If it be human thing, why does it sit gazing at me, never speaking? why does my tongue refuse to question it? why does all power forsake me in its presence, so that I stand as in a dream? Yet if it be spirit, why do I hear the passing of her feet? and why does the night-rain glisten on her hair?

"I force myself back into my chair. It is far into the night, and I am alone, waiting, listening. If it be spirit, she will come to me; and if it be woman, I shall hear her cry above the storm—unless it be a demon mocking me.

"I have heard the cry. It rose, piercing and shrill, above the storm, above the riving and rending of the bridge, above the downward crashing of the logs and loosened stones. I hear it as I listen now. It is cleaving its way upward from the depths below. It is wailing through the room as I sit writing.

"I have crawled upon my belly to the utmost edge of the still standing pier, until I could feel with my hand the jagged splinters left by the fallen planks, and have looked down. But the chasm was full to the brim with darkness. I shouted, but the wind shook my voice into mocking laughter. I sit here, feebly striking at the madness that is creeping nearer and nearer to me. I tell myself the whole thing is but the fever in my brain. The bridge was rotten. The storm was strong. The cry is but a single one among the many voices of the mountain. Yet still I listen; and it rises, clear and shrill, above the moaning of the pines, above the sobbing of the waters. It beats like blows upon my skull, and I know that she will never come again."

Extract from the last letter:

"I shall address an envelope to you, and leave it among these letters. Then, should I never come back, some chance wanderer may one day find and post them to you, and you will know.

"My books and writings remain untouched. We sit together of a night—this woman I call 'wife' and I—she holding in her hands some knitted thing that never grows longer by a single stitch, and I with a volume before me that is ever open at the same page. And day and night we watch each other stealthily, moving to and fro about the silent house; and at times, looking round swiftly, I catch the smile upon her lips before she has time to smooth it away.

We speak like strangers about this and that, making talk to hide our thoughts. We make a pretence of busying ourselves about whatever will help us to keep apart from one another.

"At night, sitting here between the shadows and the dull glow of the smouldering twigs, I sometimes think I hear the tapping I have learnt to listen for, and I start from my seat, and softly open the door and look out. But only the Night stands there. Then I close-to the latch, and she—the living woman—asks me in her purring voice what sound I heard, hiding a smile as she stoops low over her work; and I answer lightly, and, moving towards her, put my arm about her, feeling her softness and her suppleness, and wondering, supposing I held her close to me with one arm while pressing her from me with the other, how long before I should hear the cracking of her bones.

"For here, amid these savage solitudes, I also am grown savage. The old primeval passions of love and hate stir within me, and they are fierce and cruel and strong, beyond what you men of the later ages could understand. The culture of the centuries has fallen from me as a flimsy garment whirled away by the mountain wind; the old savage instincts of the race lie bare. One day I shall twine my fingers about her full white throat, and her eyes will slowly come towards me, and her lips will part, and the red tongue creep out; and backwards, step by step, I shall push her before me, gazing the while upon her bloodless face, and it will be my turn to smile. Backwards through the open door, backwards along the garden path between the juniper bushes, backwards till her heels are overhanging the ravine, and she grips life with nothing but her little toes, I shall force her, step by step, before me. Then I shall lean forward, closer, closer, till I kiss her purpling lips, and down, down, down, past the startled sea- birds, past the white spray of the foss, past the downward peeping pines, down, down, down, we will go together, till we find the thing that lies sleeping beneath the waters of the fiord."

With these words ended the last letter, unsigned. At the first streak of dawn we left the house, and, after much wandering, found our way back to the valley. But of our guide we heard no news. Whether he remained still upon the mountain, or whether by some false step he had perished upon that night, we never learnt.

Variety Patter

My first appearance at a Music Hall was in the year one thousand eight hundred and s—. Well, I would rather not mention the exact date. I was fourteen at the time. It was during the Christmas holidays, and my aunt had given me five shillings to go and see Phelps—I think it was Phelps—in *Coriolanus*—I think it was *Coriolanus*. Anyhow, it was to see a high-class and improving entertainment, I know.

I suggested that I should induce young Skegson, who lived in our road, to go with me. Skegson is a barrister now, and could not tell you the difference between a knave of clubs and a club of knaves. A few years hence he will, if he works hard, be innocent enough for a judge. But at the period of which I speak he was a red-haired boy of worldly tastes, notwithstanding which I loved him as a brother. My dear mother wished to see him before consenting to the arrangement, so as to be able to form her own opinion as to whether he was a fit and proper companion for me; and, accordingly, he was invited to tea. He came, and made a most favourable impression upon both my mother and my aunt. He had a way of talking about the advantages of application to study in early life, and the duties of youth towards those placed in authority over it, that won for him much esteem in grown-up circles. The spirit of the Bar had descended upon Skegson at a very early period of his career.

My aunt, indeed, was so much pleased with him that she gave him two shillings towards his own expenses ("sprung half a dollar" was how he explained the transaction when we were outside), and commended me to his especial care.

Skegson was very silent during the journey. An idea was evidently maturing in his mind. At the Angel he stopped and said: "Look here, I'll tell you what we'll do. Don't let's go and see that rot. Let's go to a Music Hall."

I gasped for breath. I had heard of Music Halls. A stout lady had denounced them across our dinner table on one occasion—fixing the while a steely eye upon her husband, who sat opposite and seemed uncomfortable—as low, horrid places, where people smoked and drank, and wore short skirts, and had added an opinion that they ought to be put down by the police—whether the skirts or the halls she did not explain. I also recollected that our charwoman, whose son had lately left

London for a protracted stay in Devonshire, had, in conversation with my mother, dated his downfall from the day when he first visited one of these places; and likewise that Mrs. Philcox's nursemaid, upon her confessing that she had spent an evening at one with her young man, had been called a shameless hussy, and summarily dismissed as being no longer a fit associate for the baby.

But the spirit of lawlessness was strong within me in those days, so that I hearkened to the voice of Skegson, the tempter, and he lured my feet from the paths that led to virtue and Sadler's Wells, and we wandered into the broad and crowded ways that branch off from the Angel towards Merry Islington.

Skegson insisted that we should do the thing in style, so we stopped at a shop near the Agricultural Hall and purchased some big cigars. A huge card in the window claimed for these that they were "the most satisfactory twopenny smokes in London." I smoked two of them during the evening, and never felt more satisfied—using the word in its true sense, as implying that a person has had enough of a thing, and does not desire any more of it, just then—in all my life. Where we went, and what we saw, my memory is not very clear upon. We sat at a little marble table. I know it was marble because it was so hard, and cool to the head. From out of the smoky mist a ponderous creature of strange, undefined shape floated heavily towards us, and deposited a squat tumbler in front of me containing a pale yellowish liquor, which subsequent investigation has led me to believe must have been Scotch whisky. It seemed to me then the most nauseous stuff I had ever swallowed. It is curious to look back and notice how one's tastes change.

I reached home very late and very sick. That was my first dissipation, and, as a lesson, it has been of more practical use to me than all the good books and sermons in the world could have been. I can remember to this day standing in the middle of the room in my night-shirt, trying to catch my bed as it came round.

Next morning I confessed everything to my mother, and, for several months afterwards, was a reformed character. Indeed, the pendulum of my conscience swung too far the other way, and I grew exaggeratedly remorseful and unhealthily moral.

There was published in those days, for the edification of young people, a singularly pessimistic periodical, entitled *The Children's Band of Hope Review*. It was a magazine much in favour among grown-up people, and a bound copy of Vol. IX. had lately been won by my sister as a prize for punctuality (I fancy she must have exhausted all the virtue she ever possessed, in that direction, upon the winning of that prize. At all events, I have noticed no ostentatious display of the quality in her later life.) I had formerly expressed contempt for this book, but now, in my regenerate state, I took a morbid pleasure in poring over its denunciations of sin and sinners. There was one picture in it that appeared peculiarly applicable to myself. It represented a gaudily costumed young man, standing on the topmost of three steep steps, smoking a large cigar. Behind him was a very small church, and below, a bright and not altogether uninviting looking hell. The picture was headed "The Three Steps to Ruin," and the three stairs were labelled respectively "Smoking," "Drinking," "Gambling." I had already travelled two-thirds of the road! Was I going all the way, or should I be able to retrace those steps? I used to lie awake at night and think about it till I grew half crazy. Alas! since then I have completed the descent, so where my future will be spent I do not care to think.

Another picture in the book that troubled me was the frontispiece. This was a highly-coloured print, illustrating the broad and narrow ways. The narrow way led upward past a Sunday-school and a lion to a city in the clouds. This city was referred to in the accompanying letterpress as a place of "Rest and Peace," but inasmuch as the town was represented in the illustration as surrounded by a perfect mob of angels, each one blowing a trumpet twice his own size, and obviously blowing it for all he was worth, a certain confusion of ideas would seem to have crept into the allegory.

The other path—the "broad way"—which ended in what at first glance appeared to be a highly successful display of fireworks, started from the door of a tavern, and led past a Music Hall, on the steps of which stood a gentleman smoking a cigar. All the wicked people in this book smoked cigars—all except one young man who had killed his mother and died raving mad. He had gone astray on short pipes.

This made it uncomfortably clear to me which direction I had chosen, and I was greatly alarmed, until, on examining the picture more closely, I noticed, with much satisfaction, that about midway the two paths were connected by a handy little bridge, by the use of which it seemed feasible, starting on the one path and ending up on the other, to combine the practical advantages of both roads. From subsequent observation I have come to the conclusion that a good many people have made a note of that little bridge.

My own belief in the possibility of such convenient compromise must, I fear, have led to an ethical relapse, for there recurs to my mind a somewhat painful scene of a few months' later date, in which I am seeking to convince a singularly unresponsive landed proprietor that my presence in his orchard is solely and entirely due to my having unfortunately lost my way.

It was not until I was nearly seventeen that the idea occurred to me to visit a Music Hall again. Then, having regard to my double capacity of "Man About Town" and journalist (for I had written a letter to *The Era*, complaining of the way pit doors were made to open, and it had been inserted), I felt I had no longer any right to neglect acquaintanceship with so important a feature in the life of the people. Accordingly, one Saturday night, I wended my way to the "Pav."; and there the first person that I ran against was my uncle. He laid a heavy hand upon my shoulder, and asked me, in severe tones, what I was doing there. I felt this to be an awkward question, for it would have been useless trying to make him understand my real motives (one's own relations are never sympathetic), and I was somewhat nonplussed for an answer, until the reflection occurred to me: What was *he* doing there? This riddle I, in my turn, propounded to him, with the result that we entered into treaty, by the terms of which it was agreed that no future reference should be made to the meeting by either of us—especially not in the presence of my aunt—and the compact was ratified according to the usual custom, my uncle paying the necessary expenses.

In those days, we sat, some four or six of us, round a little table, on which were placed our drinks. Now we have to balance them upon a narrow ledge; and ladies, as they pass, dip the ends of their cloaks into them, and gentlemen stir them up for us with the ferrules of their umbrellas, or else sweep them off into our laps with their coat tails, saying as they do so, "Oh, I beg your pardon."

Also, in those days, there were "chairmen"—affable gentlemen, who would drink anything at anybody's expense, and drink any quantity of it, and never seem to get any fuller. I was introduced to a Music Hall chairman once, and when I said to him, "What is your drink?" he took up the "list of beverages" that lay before him, and, opening it, waved his hand lightly across its entire contents, from clarets, past champagnes and spirits, down to liqueurs. "That's my drink, my boy," said he. There was nothing narrow-minded or exclusive about his tastes.

It was the chairman's duty to introduce the artists. "Ladies and gentlemen," he would shout, in a voice that united the musical characteristics of a foghorn and a steam saw, "Miss 'Enerietta Montressor, the popular serio-comic, will now happear." These announcements were invariably received with great applause by the chairman himself, and generally with chilling indifference by the rest of the audience.

It was also the privilege of the chairman to maintain order, and reprimand evil-doers. This he usually did very effectively, employing for the purpose language both fit and forcible. One chairman that I remember seemed, however, to be curiously deficient in the necessary qualities for this part of his duty. He was a mild and sleepy little man, and, unfortunately, he had to preside over an exceptionally rowdy audience at a small hall in the South-East district. On the night that I was present, there occurred a great disturbance. "Joss Jessop, the Monarch of Mirth," a gentleman evidently high in local request was, for some reason or other, not forthcoming, and in his place the management proposed to offer a female performer on the zithern, one Signorina Ballatino.

The little chairman made the announcement in a nervous, deprecatory tone, as if he were rather ashamed of it himself. "Ladies and gentlemen," he began,—the poor are staunch sticklers for etiquette: I overheard a small child explaining to her mother one night in Three Colts Street, Limehouse, that she could not get into the house because there was a "lady" on the doorstep, drunk,—"Signorina Ballatino, the world-renowned—"

Here a voice from the gallery requested to know what had become of "Old Joss," and was greeted by loud cries of "'Ear, 'ear."

The chairman, ignoring the interruption, continued:

"—the world-renowned performer on the zither—"

"On the whoter?" came in tones of plaintive inquiry from the back of the hall.

"*Hon* the zither," retorted the chairman, waxing mildly indignant; he meant zithern, but he called it a zither. "A hinstrument well-known to anybody as 'as 'ad any learning."

This sally was received with much favour, and a gentleman who claimed to be acquainted with the family history of the interrupter begged the chairman to excuse that ill-bred person on the ground that his mother used to get drunk with the twopence a week and never sent him to school.

Cheered by this breath of popularity, our little president endeavoured to complete his introduction of the Signorina. He again repeated that she was the world-renowned performer on the zithern; and, undeterred by the audible remark of a lady in the pit to the effect that she'd "never 'eard on 'er," added:

"She will now, ladies and gentlemen, with your kind permission, give you examples of the—"

"Blow yer zither!" here cried out the gentleman who had started the agitation; "we want Joss Jessop."

This was the signal for much cheering and shrill whistling, in the midst of which a wag with a piping voice suggested as a reason for the favourite's non-appearance that he had not been paid his last week's salary.

A temporary lull occurred at this point; and the chairman, seizing the opportunity to complete his oft-impeded speech, suddenly remarked, "songs of the Sunny South"; and immediately sat down and began hammering upon the table.

Then Signora Ballatino, clothed in the costume of the Sunny South, where clothes are less essential than in these colder climes, skipped airily forward, and was most ungallantly greeted with a storm of groans and hisses. Her beloved instrument was unfeelingly alluded to as a pie-dish, and she was advised to take it back and get the penny on it. The chairman, addressed by his Christian name of "Jimmee," was told to lie down and let her sing him to sleep. Every time she attempted to start playing, shouts were raised for Joss.

At length the chairman, overcoming his evident disinclination to take any sort of hand whatever in the game, rose and gently hinted at the desirability of silence. The suggestion not meeting with any support, he proceeded to adopt sterner measures. He addressed himself personally to the ringleader of the rioters, the man who had first championed the cause of the absent Joss. This person was a brawny individual, who, judging from appearances, followed in his business hours the calling of a coalheaver. "Yes, sir," said the chairman, pointing a finger towards him, where he sat in the front row of the gallery; "you, sir, in the flannel shirt. I can see you. Will you allow this lady to give her entertainment?"

"No," answered he of the coalheaving profession, in stentorian tones.

"Then, sir," said the little chairman, working himself up into a state suggestive of Jove about to launch a thunderbolt—"then, sir, all I can say is that you are no gentleman."

This was a little too much, or rather a good deal too little, for the Signora Ballatino. She had hitherto been standing in a meek attitude of pathetic appeal, wearing a fixed smile of ineffable sweetness but she evidently felt that she could go a bit farther than that herself, even if she was a lady. Calling the chairman "an old messer," and telling him for Gawd's sake to shut up if that was all he could do for his living, she came down to the front, and took the case into her own hands.

She did not waste time on the rest of the audience. She went direct for that coalheaver, and thereupon ensued a slanging match the memory of which sends a trill of admiration through me even to this day. It was a battle worthy of the gods. He was a heaver of coals, quick and ready beyond his kind. During many years sojourn East and South, in the course of many wanderings from Billingsgate to Limehouse Hole, from Petticoat Lane to Whitechapel Road; out of eel-pie shop and penny gaff; out of tavern and street, and court and doss-house, he had gathered together slang words and terms and phrases, and they came back to him now, and he stood up against her manfully.

But as well might the lamb stand up against the eagle, when the shadow of its wings falls across the green pastures, and the wind flies before its dark oncoming. At the end of two minutes he lay gasping, dazed, and speechless.

Then she began.

She announced her intention of "wiping down the bloomin' 'all" with him, and making it respectable; and, metaphorically speaking, that is what she did. Her tongue hit him between the eyes, and knocked him down and trampled on him. It curled round and round him like a whip, and then it uncurled and wound the other way. It seized him by the scruff of his neck, and tossed him up into the air, and caught him as he descended, and flung him to the ground, and rolled him on it. It played around him like forked lightning, and blinded him. It danced and shrieked about him like a host of whirling fiends, and he tried to remember a prayer, and could not. It touched him lightly on the sole of his foot and the crown of his head, and his hair stood up straight, and his limbs grew stiff. The people sitting near him drew away, not feeling it safe to be near, and left him alone, surrounded by space, and language.

It was the most artistic piece of work of its kind that I have ever heard. Every phrase she flung at him seemed to have been woven on purpose to entangle him and to embrace in its choking folds his people and his gods, to strangle with its threads his every hope, ambition, and belief. Each term she put upon him clung to him like a garment, and fitted him without a crease. The last name that she called him one felt to be, until one heard the next, the one name that he ought to have been christened by.

For five and three-quarter minutes by the clock she spoke, and never for one instant did she pause or falter; and in the whole of that onslaught there was only one weak spot.

That was when she offered to make a better man than he was out of a Guy Fawkes and a lump of coal. You felt that one lump of coal would not have been sufficient.

At the end, she gathered herself together for one supreme effort, and hurled at him an insult so bitter with scorn so sharp with insight into his career and character, so heavy with prophetic curse, that strong men drew and held their breath while it passed over them, and women hid their faces and shivered.

Then she folded her arms, and stood silent; and the house, from floor to ceiling, rose and cheered her until there was no more breath left in its lungs.

In that one night she stepped from oblivion into success. She is now a famous "artiste."

But she does not call herself Signora Ballatino, and she does not play upon the zithern. Her name has a homelier sound, and her speciality is the delineation of coster character.

I fear I must be of a somewhat gruesome turn of mind. My sympathies are always with the melancholy side of life and nature. I love the chill October days, when the brown leaves lie thick and sodden underneath your feet, and a low sound as of stifled sobbing is heard in the damp woods—the evenings in late autumn time, when the white mist creeps across the fields, making it seem as though old Earth, feeling the night air cold to its poor bones, were drawing ghostly bedclothes round its withered limbs. I like the twilight of the long grey street, sad with the wailing cry of the distant muffin man. One thinks of him, as, strangely mitred, he glides by through the gloom, jangling his harsh bell, as the High Priest of the pale spirit of Indigestion, summoning the devout to come forth and worship. I find a sweetness in the aching dreariness of Sabbath afternoons in genteel suburbs—in the evil-laden desolateness of waste places by the river, when the yellow fog is stealing inland across the ooze and mud, and the black tide gurgles softly round worm-eaten piles.

I love the bleak moor, when the thin long line of the winding road lies white on the darkening heath, while overhead some belated bird, vexed with itself for being out so late, scurries across the dusky sky, screaming angrily. I love the lonely, sullen lake, hidden away in mountain solitudes. I suppose it was my childhood's surroundings that instilled in me this affection for sombre hues. One of my earliest recollections is of a dreary marshland by the sea. By day, the water stood there in wide, shallow pools. But when one looked in the evening they were pools of blood that lay there.

It was a wild, dismal stretch of coast. One day, I found myself there all alone—I forget how it came about—and, oh, how small I felt amid the sky and the sea and the sandhills! I ran, and ran, and ran, but I never seemed to move; and then I cried, and screamed, louder and louder, and the circling seagulls screamed back mockingly at me. It was an "unken" spot, as they say up North.

In the far back days of the building of the world, a long, high ridge of stones had been reared up by the sea, dividing the swampy grassland from the sand. Some of these stones—"pebbles," so they called them round about—were as big as a man, and many as big as a fair-sized house; and when the sea was angry—and very prone he was to anger by that lonely shore, and very quick to wrath; often have I known him sink to sleep with a peaceful smile on his rippling waves, to wake in fierce fury before the night was spent—he would snatch up giant handfuls of these pebbles and fling and toss them here and there, till the noise of their rolling and crashing could be heard by the watchers in the village afar off.

"Old Nick's playing at marbles to-night," they would say to one another, pausing to listen. And then the women would close tight their doors, and try not to hear the sound.

Far out to sea, by where the muddy mouth of the river yawned wide, there rose ever a thin white line of surf, and underneath those crested waves there dwelt a very fearsome thing, called the Bar. I grew to hate and be afraid of this mysterious Bar, for I heard it spoken of always with bated breath, and I knew that it was very cruel to fisher folk, and hurt them so sometimes that they would cry whole days and nights together with the pain, or would sit with white scared faces, rocking themselves to and fro.

Once when I was playing among the sandhills, there came by a tall, grey woman, bending beneath a load of driftwood. She paused when nearly opposite to me, and, facing seaward, fixed her eyes upon the breaking surf above the Bar. "Ah, how I hate the sight of your white teeth!" she muttered; then turned and passed on.

Another morning, walking through the village, I heard a low wailing come from one of the cottages, while a little farther on a group of women were gathered in the roadway, talking. "Ay," said one of them, "I thought the Bar was looking hungry last night."

So, putting one and the other together, I concluded that the "Bar" must be an ogre, such as a body reads of in books, who lived in a coral castle deep below the river's mouth, and fed upon the fishermen as he caught them going down to the sea or coming home.

From my bedroom window, on moonlight nights, I could watch the silvery foam, marking the spot beneath where he lay hid; and I would stand on tip-toe, peering out, until at length I would come to fancy I could see his hideous form floating below the waters. Then, as the little white-sailed boats stole by him, tremblingly, I used to tremble too, lest he should suddenly open his grim jaws and gulp them down; and when they had all safely reached the dark, soft sea beyond, I would steal back to the bedside, and pray to God to make the Bar good, so that he would give up eating the poor fishermen.

Another incident connected with that coast lives in my mind. It was the morning after a great storm—great even for that stormy coast—and the passion-worn waters were still heaving with the memory of a fury that was dead. Old Nick had scattered his marbles far and wide, and there were rents and fissures in the pebbly wall such as the oldest fisherman had never known before. Some of the hugest stones lay tossed a hundred yards away, and the waters had dug pits here and there along the ridge so deep that a tall man might stand in some of them, and yet his head not reach the level of the sand.

Round one of these holes a small crowd was pressing eagerly, while one man, standing in the hollow, was lifting the few remaining stones off something that lay there at the bottom. I pushed my way between the straggling legs of a big fisher lad, and peered over with the rest. A ray of sunlight streamed down into the pit, and the thing at the bottom gleamed white. Sprawling there among the black pebbles it looked like a huge spider. One by one the last stones were lifted away, and the thing was left bare, and then the crowd looked at one another and shivered.

"Wonder how he got there," said a woman at length; "somebody must ha' helped him."

"Some foreign chap, no doubt," said the man who had lifted off the stones; "washed ashore and buried here by the sea."

"What, six foot below the water-mark, wi' all they stones atop of him?" said another.

"That's no foreign chap," cried a grizzled old woman, pressing forward. "What's that that's aside him?"

Some one jumped down and took it from the stone where it lay glistening, and handed it up to her, and she clutched it in her skinny hand. It was a gold earring, such as fishermen sometimes wear. But this was a somewhat large one, and of rather unusual shape.

"That's young Abram Parsons, I tell 'ee, as lies down there," cried the old creature, wildly. "I ought to know. I gave him the pair o' these forty year ago."

It may be only an idea of mine, born of after brooding upon the scene. I am inclined to think it must be so, for I was only a child at the time, and would hardly have noticed such a thing. But it seems to my remembrance that as the old crone ceased, another woman in the crowd raised her eyes slowly, and fixed them on a withered, ancient man, who leant upon a stick, and that for a moment, unnoticed by the rest, these two stood looking strangely at each other.

JEROME K. JEROME

From these sea-scented scenes, my memory travels to a weary land where dead ashes lie, and there is blackness—blackness everywhere. Black rivers flow between black banks; black, stunted trees grow in black fields; black withered flowers by black wayside. Black roads lead from blackness past blackness to blackness; and along them trudge black, savage-looking men and women; and by them black, old-looking children play grim, unchildish games.

When the sun shines on this black land, it glitters black and hard; and when the rain falls a black mist rises towards heaven, like the hopeless prayer of a hopeless soul.

By night it is less dreary, for then the sky gleams with a lurid light, and out of the darkness the red flames leap, and high up in the air they gambol and writhe—the demon spawn of that evil land, they seem.

Visitors who came to our house would tell strange tales of this black land, and some of the stories I am inclined to think were true. One man said he saw a young bull-dog fly at a boy and pin him by the throat. The lad jumped about with much sprightliness, and tried to knock the dog away. Whereupon the boy's father rushed out of the house, hard by, and caught his son and heir roughly by the shoulder. "Keep still, thee young—, can't 'ee!" shouted the man angrily; "let 'un taste blood."

Another time, I heard a lady tell how she had visited a cottage during a strike, to find the baby, together with the other children, almost dying for want of food. "Dear, dear me!" she cried, taking the wee wizened mite from the mother's arms, "but I sent you down a quart of milk, yesterday. Hasn't the child had it?"

"Theer weer a little coom, thank 'ee kindly, ma'am," the father took upon himself to answer; "but thee see it weer only just enow for the poops."

We lived in a big lonely house on the edge of a wide common. One night, I remember, just as I was reluctantly preparing to climb into bed, there came a wild ringing at the gate, followed by a hoarse, shrieking cry, and then a frenzied shaking of the iron bars.

Then hurrying footsteps sounded through the house, and the swift opening and closing of doors; and I slipped back hastily into my knickerbockers and ran out. The women folk were gathered on the stairs, while my father stood in the hall, calling to them to be quiet. And still the wild ringing of the bell continued, and, above it, the hoarse, shrieking cry.

My father opened the door and went out, and we could hear him striding down the gravel path, and we clung to one another and waited.

After what seemed an endless time, we heard the heavy gate unbarred, and quickly clanged to, and footsteps returning on the gravel. Then the door opened again, and my father entered, and behind him a crouching figure that felt its way with its hands as it crept along, as a blind man might. The figure stood up when it reached the middle of the hall, and mopped its eyes with a dirty rag that it carried in its hand; after which it held the rag over the umbrella-stand and wrung it out, as washerwomen wring out clothes, and the dark drippings fell into the tray with a dull, heavy splut.

My father whispered something to my mother, and she went out towards the back; and, in a little while, we heard the stamping of hoofs—the angry plunge of a spur-startled horse—the rhythmic throb of the long, straight gallop, dying away into the distance.

My mother returned and spoke some reassuring words to the servants. My father, having made fast the door and extinguished all but one or two of the lights, had gone into a small room on the right of the hall; the crouching figure, still mopping that moisture from its eyes, following him. We could hear them talking there in low tones, my father questioning, the other voice thick and interspersed with short panting grunts.

We on the stairs huddled closer together, and, in the darkness, I felt my mother's arm steal round me and encompass me, so that I was not afraid. Then we waited, while the silence round our frightened whispers thickened and grew heavy till the weight of it seemed to hurt us.

At length, out of its depths, there crept to our ears a faint murmur. It gathered strength like the sound of the oncoming of a wave upon a stony shore, until it broke in a Babel of vehement voices just outside. After a few moments, the hubbub ceased, and there came a furious ringing—then angry shouts demanding admittance.

Some of the women began to cry. My father came out into the hall, closing the room door behind him, and ordered them to be quiet, so sternly that they were stunned into silence. The furious ringing was repeated; and, this time, threats mingled among the hoarse shouts. My mother's arm tightened around me, and I could hear the beating of her heart.

The voices outside the gate sank into a low confused mumbling. Soon they died away altogether, and the silence flowed back.

My father turned up the hall lamp, and stood listening.

Suddenly, from the back of the house, rose the noise of a great crashing, followed by oaths and savage laughter.

My father rushed forward, but was borne back; and, in an instant, the hall was full of grim, ferocious faces. My father, trembling a little (or else it was the shadow cast by the flickering lamp), and with lips tight pressed, stood confronting them; while we women and children, too scared to even cry, shrank back up the stairs.

What followed during the next few moments is, in my memory, only a confused tumult, above which my father's high, clear tones rise every now and again, entreating, arguing, commanding. I see nothing distinctly until one of the grimmest of the faces thrusts itself before the others, and a voice which, like Aaron's rod, swallows up all its fellows, says in deep, determined bass, "Coom, we've had enow chatter, master. Thee mun give 'un up, or thee mun get out o' th' way an' we'll search th' house for oursel'."

Then a light flashed into my father's eyes that kindled something inside me, so that the fear went out of me, and I struggled to free myself from my mother's arm, for the desire stirred me to fling myself down upon the grimy faces below, and beat and stamp upon them with my fists. Springing across the hall, he snatched from the wall where it hung an ancient club, part of a trophy of old armour, and planting his back against the door through which they would have to pass, he shouted, "Then be damned to you all, he's in this room! Come and fetch him out."

(I recollect that speech well. I puzzled over it, even at that time, excited though I was. I had always been told that only low, wicked people ever used the word "damn," and I tried to reconcile things, and failed.)

The men drew back and muttered among themselves. It was an ugly-looking weapon, studded with iron spikes. My father held it secured to his hand by a chain, and there was an ugly look about him also, now, that gave his face a strange likeness to the dark faces round him.

But my mother grew very white and cold, and underneath her breath she kept crying, "Oh, will they never come—will they never come?" and a cricket somewhere about the house began to chirp.

Then all at once, without a word, my mother flew down the stairs, and passed like a flash of light through the crowd of dusky figures. How she did it I could never understand, for the two heavy bolts had both been drawn, but the next moment the door stood wide open; and a hum of voices, cheery with the anticipation of a period of perfect bliss, was borne in upon the cool night air.

My mother was always very quick of hearing.

AGAIN, I SEE A WILD crowd of grim faces, and my father's, very pale, amongst them. But this time the faces are very many, and they come and go like faces in a dream. The ground beneath my feet is wet and sloppy, and a black rain is falling. There are women's faces in the crowd, wild and haggard, and long skinny arms stretch out threateningly towards my father, and shrill, frenzied voices call out curses on him. Boys' faces also pass me in the grey light, and on some of them there is an impish grin.

I seem to be in everybody's way; and to get out of it, I crawl into a dark, draughty corner and crouch there among cinders. Around me, great engines fiercely strain and pant like living things fighting beyond their strength. Their gaunt arms whirl madly above me, and the ground rocks with their throbbing. Dark figures flit to and fro, pausing from time to time to wipe the black sweat from their faces.

The pale light fades, and the flame-lit night lies red upon the land. The flitting figures take strange shapes. I hear the hissing of wheels, the furious clanking of iron chains, the hoarse shouting of many voices, the hurrying tread of many feet; and, through all, the wailing and weeping and cursing that never seem to cease. I drop into a restless sleep, and dream that I have broken a chapel window, stone-throwing, and have died and gone to hell.

At length, a cold hand is laid upon my shoulder, and I awake. The wild faces have vanished and all is silent now, and I wonder if the whole thing has been a dream. My father lifts me into the dog-cart, and we drive home through the chill dawn.

My mother opens the door softly as we alight. She does not speak, only looks her question. "It's all over, Maggie," answers my father very quietly, as he takes off his coat and lays it across a chair; "we've got to begin the world afresh."

My mother's arms steal up about his neck; and I, feeling heavy with a trouble I do not understand, creep off to bed.

The Lease of the "Cross Keys"

This story is about a shop: many stories are. One Sunday evening this Bishop had to preach a sermon at St. Paul's Cathedral. The occasion was a very special and important one, and every God-fearing newspaper in the kingdom sent its own special representative to report the proceedings.

Now, of the three reporters thus commissioned, one was a man of appearance so eminently respectable that no one would have thought of taking him for a journalist. People used to put him down for a County Councillor or an Archdeacon at the very least. As a matter of fact, however, he was a sinful man, with a passion for gin. He lived at Bow, and, on the Sabbath in question, he left his home at five o'clock in the afternoon, and started to walk to the scene of his labours. The road from Bow to the City on a wet and chilly Sunday evening is a cheerless one; who can blame him if on his way he stopped once or twice to comfort himself with "two" of his favourite beverage? On reaching St. Paul's he found he had twenty minutes to spare—just time enough for one final "nip." Half way down a narrow court leading out of the Churchyard he found a quiet little hostelry, and, entering the private bar, whispered insinuatingly across the counter:

"Two of gin hot, if you please, my dear."

His voice had the self-satisfied meekness of the successful ecclesiastic, his bearing suggested rectitude tempered by desire to avoid observation. The barmaid, impressed by his manner and appearance, drew the attention of the landlord to him. The landlord covertly took stock of so much of him as could be seen between his buttoned-up coat and his drawn-down hat, and wondered how so bland and innocent-looking a gentleman came to know of gin.

A landlord's duty, however, is not to wonder, but to serve. The gin was given to the man, and the man drank it. He liked it. It was good gin: he was a connoisseur, and he knew. Indeed, so good did it seem to him that he felt it would be a waste of opportunity not to have another twopen'orth. Therefore he had a second "go"; maybe a third. Then he returned to the Cathedral, and sat himself down with his notebook on his knee and waited.

As the service proceeded there stole over him that spirit of indifference to all earthly surroundings that religion and drink are alone able to bestow. He heard the good Bishop's text and wrote it down. Then he heard the Bishop's "sixthly and lastly," and took that down, and looked at his notebook and wondered in a peaceful way what had become of the "firstly" to "fifthly" inclusive. He sat there wondering until the people round him began to get up and move away, whereupon it struck him swiftly and suddenly that he had been asleep, and had thereby escaped the main body of the discourse.

What on earth was he to do? He was representing one of the leading religious papers. A full report of the sermon was wanted that very night. Seizing the robe of a passing wandsman, he tremulously inquired if the Bishop had yet left the Cathedral. The wandsman answered that he had not, but that he was just on the point of doing so.

"I must see him before he goes!" exclaimed the reporter, excitedly.

"You can't," replied the wandsman. The journalist grew frantic.

"Tell him," he cried, "a penitent sinner desires to speak with him about the sermon he has just delivered. To-morrow it will be too late."

The wandsman was touched; so was the Bishop. He said he would see the poor fellow.

As soon as the door was shut the man, with tears in his eyes, told the Bishop the truth—leaving out the gin. He said that he was a poor man, and not in good health, that he had been up half the night before, and had walked all the way from Bow that evening. He dwelt on the disastrous results to himself and his family should he fail to obtain a report of the sermon. The Bishop felt sorry for the man. Also, he was anxious that his sermon should be reported.

"Well, I trust it will be a warning to you against going to sleep in church," he said, with an indulgent smile. "Luckily, I have brought my notes with me, and if you will promise to be very careful of them, and to bring them back to me the first thing in the morning, I will lend them to you."

With this, the Bishop opened and handed to the man a neat little black leather bag, inside which lay a neat little roll of manuscript.

"Better take the bag to keep it in," added the Bishop. "Be sure and let me have them both back early to-morrow."

The reporter, when he examined the contents of the bag under a lamp in the Cathedral vestibule, could hardly believe his good fortune. The careful Bishop's notes were so full and clear that for all practical purposes they were equal to a report. His work was already done. He felt so pleased with himself that he determined to treat himself to another "two" of gin, and, with this intent, made his way across to the little "public" before-mentioned.

"It's really excellent gin you sell here," he said to the barmaid when he had finished; "I think, my dear, I'll have just one more."

At eleven the landlord gently but firmly insisted on his leaving, and he went, assisted, as far as the end of the court, by the potboy. After he was gone, the landlord noticed a neat little black bag on the seat where he had been lying. Examining it closely, he discovered a brass plate between the handles, and upon the brass plate were engraved the owner's name and title. Opening the bag, the landlord saw a neat little roll of manuscript, and across a corner of the manuscript was written the Bishop's name and address.

The landlord blew a long, low whistle, and stood with his round eyes wide open gazing down at the open bag. Then he put on his hat and coat, and taking the bag, went out down the court, chuckling hugely as he walked. He went straight to the house of the Resident Canon and rang the bell.

"Tell Mr.—," he said to the servant, "that I must see him to-night. I wouldn't disturb him at this late hour if it wasn't something very important."

The landlord was ushered up. Closing the door softly behind him, he coughed deferentially.

"Well, Mr. Peters" (I will call him "Peters"), said the Canon, "what is it?"

"Well, sir," said Mr. Peters, slowly and deliberately, "it's about that there lease o' mine. I do hope you gentlemen will see your way to makin' it twenty-one year instead o' fourteen."

"God bless the man!" cried the Canon, jumping up indignantly, "you don't mean to say you've come to me at eleven o'clock on a Sunday night to talk about your lease?"

"Well, not entirely, sir," answered Peters, unabashed; "there's another little thing I wished to speak to you about, and that's this"—saying which, he laid the Bishop's bag before the Canon and told his story.

The Canon looked at Mr. Peters, and Mr. Peters looked at the Canon.

"There must be some mistake," said the Canon.

"There's no mistake," said the landlord. "I had my suspicions when I first clapped eyes on him. I seed he wasn't our usual sort, and I seed how he tried to hide his face. If he weren't the Bishop, then I don't know a

Bishop when I sees one, that's all. Besides, there's his bag, and there's his sermon."

Mr. Peters folded his arms and waited. The Canon pondered. Such things had been known to happen before in Church history. Why not again?

"Does any one know of this besides yourself?" asked the Canon.

"Not a livin' soul," replied Mr. Peters, "as yet."

"I think—I think, Mr. Peters," said the Canon, "that we may be able to extend your lease to twenty-one years."

"Thank you kindly, sir," said the landlord, and departed. Next morning the Canon waited on the Bishop and laid the bag before him.

"Oh," said the Bishop cheerfully, "he's sent it back by you, has he?"

"He has, sir," replied the Canon; "and thankful I am that it was to me he brought it. It is right," continued the Canon, "that I should inform your lordship that I am aware of the circumstances under which it left your hands."

The Canon's eye was severe, and the Bishop laughed uneasily.

"I suppose it wasn't quite the thing for me to do," he answered apologetically; "but there, all's well that ends well," and the Bishop laughed.

This stung the Canon. "Oh, sir," he exclaimed, with a burst of fervour, "in Heaven's name—for the sake of our Church, let me entreat—let me pray you never to let such a thing occur again."

The Bishop turned upon him angrily.

"Why, what a fuss you make about a little thing!" he cried; then, seeing the look of agony upon the other's face, he paused.

"How did you get that bag?" he asked.

"The landlord of the Cross Keys brought it me," answered the Canon; "you left it there last night."

The Bishop gave a gasp, and sat down heavily. When he recovered his breath, he told the Canon the real history of the case; and the Canon is still trying to believe it.

A Note About the Author

Born Jerome Clapp, English author and humorist Jerome K. Jerome (1859–1927) later changed his last name to mirror his first. As a child, Jerome dreamed of a career in politics, but was forced to quit his studies and find a job at age thirteen after his father passed away. Jerome worked various jobs, including working on the railway, joining a traveling acting company for three years, and volunteering as an ambulance driver for the French army. In 1888, he married Georgina Marris, and had one stepchild from his wife's previous marriage. Jerome earned success with his comedic work, including his novel *Three Men in a Boat*.

A Note from the Publisher

Spanning many genres, from non-fiction essays to literature classics to children's books and lyric poetry, Mint Edition books showcase the master works of our time in a modern new package. The text is freshly typeset, is clean and easy to read, and features a new note about the author in each volume. Many books also include exclusive new introductory material. Every book boasts a striking new cover, which makes it as appropriate for collecting as it is for gift giving. Mint Edition books are only printed when a reader orders them, so natural resources are not wasted. We're proud that our books are never manufactured in excess and exist only in the exact quantity they need to be read and enjoyed.

bookfinity™

Discover more of your favorite classics with Bookfinity™.

- Track your reading with custom book lists.
- Get great book recommendations for your personalized Reader Type.
- Add reviews for your favorite books.
- AND MUCH MORE!

Visit **bookfinity.com** and take the fun Reader Type quiz to get started.

Enjoy our classic and modern companion pairings!